W9-AZF-325

Beans on the Roof

Also by Betsy Byars

THE ANIMAL, THE VEGETABLE,
& JOHN D JONES
THE NIGHT SWIMMERS

The Blossom Family Quartet

THE NOT-JUST-ANYBODY FAMILY
THE BLOSSOMS MEET THE VULTURE LADY
THE BLOSSOMS AND THE GREEN PHANTOM
A BLOSSOM PROMISE

Beans on the Roof

Betsy Byars

Illustrated by Melodye Rosales

Delacorte
Press

Published by
Delacorte Press
The Bantam Doubleday Dell Publishing Group, Inc.
666 Fifth Avenue
New York, New York 10103

LIBRARY OF CONGRESS CATALOGING IN PUBLICATION DATA

Byars, Betsy Cromer.
Beans on the roof / by Betsy Byars; illustrated by Melodye Rosales.
p. cm.
Summary: As each of the five members of the Bean family tries to write a "roof" poem, they come to realize just how nice it is to be a Bean.
ISBN 0-440-50055-9
[1. Family life—Fiction. 2. Poetry—Fiction.] I. Rosales, Melodye, ill. II. Title.
PZ7.B9836Be 1988
[Fic]—dc19 88-6907
CIP
AC

Manufactured in the United States of America

October 1988

10 9 8 7 6 5 4 3 2 1

BG

Contents

Beans on the Roof

A Bean on the Roof

"Mama!"

George ran into the kitchen.

"Mama!"

"Please don't shout, George," Mrs. Bean said.

"I have to shout! You have to hear this! Anna is on the roof! I saw her from Frankie's window!"

"I know Anna is on the roof," Mrs. Bean said.

"But you told us never to play on the roof. You said we'd bother Mr. Brown's rabbits. You said we'd run into the clotheslines and dirty the clothes."

"Anna is not playing, George," Mrs. Bean said. "Anna is sitting."

"Oh."

George stopped. Then he said quickly, "I'm going up there and sit too."

George had wanted to play on the roof since the day they moved into the apartment.

"No, George," Mrs. Bean said.

George put his hands on his hips.

"Why not?" he said. "That's not fair. Anna gets to do everything. She gets to stay up late. She gets to ride the bus. Now she gets to sit on the roof. It's not fair!"

"George, will you be quiet and listen? Anna is on the roof because it is the only place she can write her poem."

George's mouth fell open.

"Anna is writing a poem?"

"That's right, George."

"I didn't know Anna knew how to write a poem."

"Yes, Anna is writing a poem. If the poem is good, it will be in a book at her school."

"A real book?"

"Yes, Anna will be the first Bean to be in a book. I want everybody to leave her alone."

George thought fast. He said, "Can I go up on the roof if I write a poem?"

"No."

"Why not, Mama? That's really not fair."

"If you want to write a poem, George, you can do it at the table."

George groaned.

"Here is a piece of paper, George. Here is a pencil."

George said, "Why does Anna get to write on the roof and I have to write at the table?"

"Anna's poem is a roof poem. Yours is not."

George sat down at the table. He thought.

He twirled his pencil. He bit it. He admired his teeth prints in the wood. He thought some more.

Finally he sighed. "I can't write a poem at the table. I'm sorry. I just can't. I have to be on the roof, like Anna."

Mrs. Bean gave in.

"All right," she said. "You may go up on the roof and write one poem. But you must not bother Anna."

"I won't."

"I mean it. Anna is the first Bean to be in a book."

"I won't bother her," George said.

He crossed his heart.

"And thank you very much, Mama."

George ran out of the apartment. He ran up the steps. He pushed open the door and stepped onto the roof.

Clean clothes snapped in the wind. Pigeons cooed in their cages. Rabbits hopped in theirs.

George took a deep breath of good roof air.

This was the place to write a poem. And George was going to write the best poem in the whole world.

Two Beans on the Roof

George sat down.

He said softly, "Hello, Anna."

Anna did not answer. She was looking across the rooftops. George said, "Mama said I could come up and write a poem too."

Anna did not answer.

George said, "I can write a poem *if* I don't bother you. And I won't bother you, Anna. I promise."

Anna closed her eyes.

"I won't bother you, no matter what."

George watched Anna. Then he closed his eyes too.

It worked. He finished his poem at once.

"I am going to write my poem down," he

said. "That way I will always have it. I will never, ever forget it."

George bent over his paper.

"You ought to write yours down too, Anna. That way you will always have it. You will never, ever forget it."

George printed his poem on the paper. He was glad he could spell all the words. He did not have to bother Anna at all.

This was George's poem:

The cat was fat.
It sat on a hat.
The hat got flat.

Then he wrote:

A poem by George (String) Bean.

The kids at school called George *String Bean.* They called his sister Jenny *Jelly Bean.* They called Anna *Anna.*

George was very happy with his poem. He read it three times to himself.

"Want to hear my poem?" George asked.

Anna was looking across the rooftops.

"It's not a long poem, Anna, and it's a funny poem. It will make you laugh."

George laughed thinking about it.

"Do you want to hear it, Anna—yes or no?"

Anna didn't answer.

Finally George got tired of waiting. He said, "Well, here goes, ready or not."

He held up his paper. He began to read:

The cat was fat.
It sat—

"Mama," Anna yelled, "String's bothering me."

Mrs. Bean stuck her head out the window. "Now, Anna," she called, "you know I don't like you to call your brother *String.* His name is George."

Anna said, "All right, *George* is bothering me, Mama."

"That's better."

"I can't write a poem with *George* reciting his junk."

George jumped up.

"Mama, it is not junk! It is a poem! It rhymes."

"It may rhyme," Anna said, "and it may be a poem. However, it is not a poem that has to be written on the roof. You could write a poem like that anywhere."

"I could not! I tried to write it at the table. Mama saw me. I tried and I could not write one word."

"I will show you a roof poem," Anna said. "This is a roof poem."

Mrs. Bean called, "Anna, if you're going

to say your poem, please say it real loud. I want to hear it."

"I will, Mama."

Anna stood up. She held her head high. She said her poem good and loud:

From my roof
I can see
Beyond the town,
Beyond the sea,
Beyond Africa,
Asia, too—

Anna stopped. "That's all I've got so far, Mama," she said. "I have to think of something that rhymes with *too.*"

"Goo, boo, cuckoo," said George.

"Do your own poem," Anna said.

"I did!"

"The cat poem does not count. If you can't do a roof poem, you have to go downstairs, and write at the table. Isn't that right, Mama?"

George said quickly, "My cat poem was a practice poem. Now I will do my real poem. It will be a roof poem."

To himself he said, And it will be the best roof poem in the whole world. It will even be better than Anna's.

He turned his paper over. He twirled his pencil. He bit it. He admired his teeth prints in the wood.

He closed his eyes to think.

Three Beans on the Roof

George got up. "I need a break," he told Anna. "This is hard work."

George walked to the side of the roof. He looked over the wall.

His sister Jenny was on the sidewalk below. Jenny was jumping rope.

Instead of "Teddy Bear, Teddy Bear," Jenny was saying:

Jelly Bean, Jelly Bean,
Turn around.
Jelly Bean, Jelly Bean,
Touch the ground.
Jelly Bean, Jelly Bean,

Shine your shoes.
Jelly Bean, Jelly Bean,
Read the news.

George yelled, "Jelly Bean! Look where I am!"

"Time out," Jenny said. She stopped jumping and looked up at the roof of her apartment building.

George said, "Hello down there."

Jenny said, "String, is that you on the roof?"

George said, "It's not Santa Claus."

Jenny said, "String Bean, you know we are not allowed on the roof. I'm going to tell Mama."

Jenny ran upstairs and into the kitchen.

"Mama!"

"Don't shout, Jenny," Mrs. Bean said.

"I have to shout! You have to hear this! String is playing on the roof!"

2500

Mrs. Bean said, "Jenny, I asked you not to call your brother *String.*"

"I forgot. I'll start over. *George* is playing on the roof."

"That's better. Both George and Anna are on the roof, Jenny, but they are not playing."

"They aren't?"

"No."

"Then what are they doing?"

"They are writing roof poems."

Jenny's mouth fell open. "I didn't know they could write roof poems, Mama."

"Yes, they can."

"George too?"

"George is trying. The only place a Bean can write roof poems is on the roof."

"Can I go up and write a poem?" Jenny asked quickly.

Jenny held her breath. After she wrote her poem, she would recite it for the rabbits. And the pigeons. It would be like a play! She was sure the rabbits and the pigeons had never seen a play.

"Oh, I guess so," Mrs. Bean said. "But it has got to be a roof poem. Otherwise, you write at the table."

"It will be a roof poem," said Jenny. "That is a promise." She crossed her heart.

"And don't bother Anna."

"I won't. That's another promise."

"Or the pigeons or the rabbits."

"I won't. That's—" Jenny stopped. "Does that mean I can't say my poem for them?"

"Well . . ."

"Please, Mama, they never get to hear poems."

"All right."

Jenny stopped at the door. "And, Mama . . ."

"What?"

"Thank you very, very much."

Jenny ran up the steps. She pushed open the door. she stepped out on the roof. She took a breath of good roof air.

Sheets snapped in the wind. Pigeons cooed. Rabbits hopped. Jenny smiled.

"I'm here, everybody," she said. "Mama says I can write a roof poem too!"

"It's not easy," George warned.

Four Beans on the Roof

Jenny ran to the edge of the roof. She called to her friends, "I can't jump rope anymore. I have to write a poem. Bye!"

Then she sat down between Anna and George.

She said to George, "I love it up here. I am on top of the world."

She said to Anna, "This was a wonderful idea, Anna. I love being on the roof."

Anna frowned. She said, "Jenny, I thought you came up here to write a poem."

"I did."

"Then write it."

"I did."

"You've already written your poem?" George asked in surprise.

George's cat poem had come fast. His roof poem had not come at all.

"Yes," said Jenny. "Do want to hear it?"

"I do," George said quickly.

"Here goes," Jenny said:

> I love the roof,
> And that's the truth.

"It's short," George said.

"I like short poems," Jenny said.

"But it doesn't rhyme."

"It does when I say it," Jenny said.

Jenny was missing two front teeth. She said her poem again to show that it did rhyme:

> I love the roof,
> And that's the troof.

Then she said, "See?"

Anna said, "Yes. Now stop bothering me."

Jenny got up. She went over to the rabbit cage. She said, "Want to hear my poem, rabbits? You too, pigeons?"

George said, "Mama said not to bother the rabbits and the pigeons."

"I'm reciting a poem for them. That is not bothering them." She grinned. "Come on, String, you can be my announcer."

"Oh, all right." George got up. He said to Anna, "I'll do my poem later." Then he went to the cages.

"Announce it the way they do on the radio, String. Say—"

"I know what to say. I listen to the radio too." George cleared his throat. "Ladies and gentlemen!"

"It would be better if you said, Rabbits and—"

George said, "Rabbits and gentlemen!"

"Not Rabbits and gentlemen! String, you're making me laugh. I won't be able to say my poem. Rabbits and pigeons!"

"Oh, all right! But this is the last time I'm doing it. Rabbits and pigeons! Here is a Bean saying a poem!"

"Thank you." Jenny Bean stepped forward. She said:

I love the roof,
And that's the troof.

"String!" a voice called. It was Frankie at the window across the street. "What are you guys doing on the roof?"

Jenny called back, "Oh, Frankie, we're having so much fun. We're making up poems."

"Don't tell him that!" George said. "Don't—" He broke off. He went and sat down by Anna. His face was red.

Frankie said, "String is writing a po-em? String, can I hear your po-em?"

George didn't answer.

"Can I come over and do a po-em?"

Mrs. Bean heard Frankie. She stuck her head out the window. "No, Frankie, you can't come over. Only Beans on the roof."

Frankie said, "Yes, Mrs. Bean."

"And," Mrs. Bean went on, "the word is *poem,* Frankie. Not *po-em.*"

"Yes, Mrs. Bean." Frankie moved back from the window. Mrs. Bean did too.

Suddenly Jenny said, "Mama!"

"What? What happened?"

Mrs. Bean put her head out the window again.

"Nothing happened—I just had a wonderful idea. I want you to come up on the roof and write a poem."

"Me?"

"Yes, Mama."

"Why, I could never write a poem. I didn't even get to finish school."

"Come on, Mama," George said. "I will help you, and you can help me."

"Yes, Mama, please try," Anna said.

Mrs. Bean said, "Oh, all right."

She came up the stairs, wiping her hands on her apron.

Mrs. Bean stepped on the roof. She went over to the clothesline. She felt her clothes to see if they were dry. Then she sat down with Jenny, George, and Anna. She looked up at the sky. She smiled.

"I've got mine," she said.

"Already?" asked George.

"Yes. Do you want to hear it?"

"Of course, Mama," said Anna.

"Please," said Jenny.

"I guess so," said George.

"Well, if you really want to." Mrs. Bean stood up. "Here it is."

When I am on the roof with
George Bean,
Jenny Bean,
and Anna Bean,
I feel like a queen.

Mrs. Bean sat down. "It's not a great poem," she said, "but it is a true one."

"It is a beautiful poem, Mama," Anna said.

"Very, very beautiful," said Jenny.

"I liked it too," George admitted.

Now, George thought, I am the only Bean in the whole world who does not have a roof poem.

Five Beans on the Roof

"Beans! Yoo-hoo! Where are you?"

It was Mr. Bean. He was home from the store. Mr. Bean sold fruit and vegetables.

"Sam," Mrs. Bean called back. "We're up here on the roof."

"The roof?"

Mr. Bean came up the stairs.

"Yes, Sam. We've been saying roof poems. Please come up and say one. It's so much fun."

Mr. Bean stuck his head out the door.

"Yes, Papa," said Anna, "I would love to hear you say a roof poem."

"No, no," said Mr. Bean. "I don't want to say a roof poem. I want to sing one."

Mr. Bean had a good singing voice. He sang along with the radio at night.

"That would be wonderful, Papa," Anna said.

"Oh, yes, Papa, please sing one," Jenny said.

"I want to hear it too," George said. He hoped it would give him an idea.

Mr. Bean came out on the roof.

Jenny said, "Wait, Papa. You want George to announce you?"

George groaned. "Please don't make me do any more announcing."

Mr. Bean smiled. "I will announce myself. Here is Sam Bean singing a song for his beautiful children."

Mr. Bean held out his hands as if they were full of gifts. Then he put one hand over his heart.

"Oh, Sam," said Mrs. Bean.

When Mr. Bean put one hand over his heart, he really meant what he was saying.

Mr. Bean stood taller. He said again, "For my beautiful children."

He cleared his throat and sang:

I LOVE your mother!
I LOVE your mother!
I LOVE your mother!
On the roof or off!

"Sam!" said Mrs. Bean.

Her cheeks got pink.

"Not so loud, Papa," said Anna. She glanced around to see if anyone was looking out the window.

George glanced at Frankie's window.

"Why not?" said Mr. Bean. "It is true."

I LOVE your mother!
I LOVE—

Mrs. Bean's cheeks got pinker. She jumped up.

"We have been out here long enough," she said. She hid her smile with her hand. "I have got to get supper."

Mrs. Bean started for the door.

"I will help, love," Mr. Bean said.

"Me too," said Jenny.

"I'll set the table," said Anna.

Mrs. Bean turned. "But, Anna, don't you want to finish your poem?"

"I'll finish it tomorrow."

"George, are you coming?" Jenny asked.

"In a minute," George said.

George felt terrible. He really was the only Bean without a roof poem.

He sat down. He closed his eyes.

Then he tried it with his eyes open. He tried crossing his legs. He tried lying down and looking up at the sky.

Nothing worked.

The sheets blew in the wind. The pigeons cooed. The rabbits hopped.

It started getting dark. George started getting cold.

"George," his mother called.

"What?"

"Come in now. Supper's almost ready."

"I haven't got my roof poem." George's voice shook a little.

"You can write it tomorrow," Mrs. Bean said. "And, George, would you please bring in the clothes?"

"Mama, I haven't got my poem!"

"Bring in the clothes for your mother, George," Mr. Bean called.

George took the clothes off the line. Then he went downstairs.

He sat at the table with the other Beans.

He ate with the other Beans.

But for the first time in his life, George didn't feel like a Bean himself.

One Bean on the Roof

"String!"

It was the next day. George was back on the roof. He was alone.

"String! String Bean!"

George looked across the street. Frankie was in the window.

"What you doing?" Frankie yelled.

George did not answer.

"Still writing your po-em?"

George frowned. It was hard to write a poem. It was impossible to write one with Frankie watching him.

"You want to play ball?" Frankie yelled. "Or would you rather write your po-em?"

Mrs. Bean heard Frankie. She called out the window. "He can't play ball, Frankie. It's too close to suppertime." Then she added, "And the word is not *po-em.* It's *poem.*"

Frankie said, "Yes, Mrs. Bean." Then he went back into his apartment.

Mrs. Bean said to Jenny, "I thought I asked you to go up and get George."

"I did, but he won't come. He wants to finish his roof poem."

"Tell him he can finish it later."

"He won't listen to me, Mama. I told him there were lots of people—important people—who didn't have roof poems. I told him George Washington didn't have a roof poem. I told him Abraham Lincoln didn't have one either."

"And he still wouldn't come down?"

"He said George Washington and Abra-

ham Lincoln didn't need roof poems. He said they weren't Beans."

Mrs. Bean stuck her head out the window again.

"George," she said. "Come down here this minute."

"But, Mama—" George began.

Frankie called from his window. "Mrs. Bean, he doesn't have his po-em yet. I mean, his poem."

Mrs. Bean said, "That's better, Frankie. George, come down this minute."

"Yes, Mama."

George came down the steps and into the kitchen.

"Nothing?" asked Jenny.

"Nothing," said George.

"Well, don't feel bad," Jenny said. "Anna hasn't finished her poem either."

"Oh, yes, I have!" Anna said.

Anna danced into the kitchen. "I have finished! After supper I will read my poem to the family."

Mr. Bean came into the kitchen then too. He said, "I cannot wait until after supper."

"But, Papa—"

"I love all the Bean poems. I have learned them by heart." He smiled at Jenny:

> I love the roof,
> And that's the troof.

He smiled at Mrs. Bean:

> When I am on the roof with
> George Bean,
> Jenny Bean,
> and Anna Bean,
> I feel like a queen.

"And my own." He threw back his head and sang:

I LOVE your mother!
I LOVE your mother!
I LOVE your mother!
On the roof or off!

"Now," he went on, "I want to hear Anna's poem so I can learn it too."

"You might as well read it, Anna," Mrs. Bean said. "Your father won't eat until he hears it."

"It can wait," Anna said.

"No, read it," Mrs. Bean said. "You have made us all so proud. You will be the first Bean to ever be in a book."

"Mama," said Anna, "my poem is not in the book yet. The teacher is going to pick the ones to go in the book."

"She'll pick yours," Jenny said. "It is the best poem in the world."

"I think she'll pick it too," said George.

George felt worse than ever. He had been up on the roof two afternoons. He still did not have a roof poem. And his father had not even asked about his poem.

George was beginning to hate poems.

"All right. If you really want to hear it, here goes."

Anna unfolded her paper:

From my roof
I can see
Beyond the town,
Beyond the sea,
Beyond Africa,
Asia, too,
Beyond another sea of blue,
Another land,
And there I find

The loveliest sight—
This roof of mine.

"My daughter can see all the way around the world," Mr. Bean said. He blew his nose.

"It is so beautiful it makes me want to cry," Mrs. Bean said. She wiped her eyes on her apron.

George looked sad too.

"You must write it down for me," Mr. Bean said. "I will put it to music. I will sing it."

"She does not have to write it down," Mrs. Bean said. "It will be in the book. You can learn it from the book!"

"Now, Mama," Anna said, "it has not been picked yet."

"It will be," Mrs. Bean said.

Anna folded the sheet of paper. "We hand

them in tomorrow," she said, crossing her fingers. "Wish me luck."

"Oh, we do. We all do." Mrs. Bean kissed Anna and hugged her. "To think of it—a Bean in a book."

With a proud smile, she wiped her eyes again.

"Wish me luck too," George said.

A Bean in the Bedroom

Anna Bean ran up the stairs. She ran through the living room. She ran into the bedroom. She shut the door.

"Anna?" Mrs. Bean said. "Is that you?"

Anna did not answer.

"Anna?"

Mrs. Bean came out of the kitchen. She was drying her hands on her apron. She went down the hall. She knocked on the door.

"Anna?"

Anna said, "Please leave me alone."

Mrs. Bean said, "Anna, are you all right?"

"Yes."

"Is there anything I can do for you?"

"No, just please leave me alone."

Mrs. Bean went back into the kitchen. She was standing at the sink when George came in.

"Do you know what's wrong with Anna?" she asked.

George shook his head.

He started into the hall, and Mrs. Bean said quickly, "Don't go in the bedroom."

"But I need my piece of paper," George said. "I'm going up on the roof to work on my poem."

"Here is a sheet of paper."

"But this has writing on it, Mama. I need my own paper."

"George, I don't want you bothering Anna. Something is wrong with Anna. I don't think she feels good."

"Oh, all right, but I need a pencil too."

"Here."

George looked at the pencil. It wasn't as good as his old one. It didn't have his teeth marks in it.

"If it starts raining, George, you come inside."

"I will."

George went slowly up the stairs to the roof.

He sat down. He stared at the sheet of paper. He stared up at the sky.

It was not a good day to be on the roof. There was no sun. No clean clothes flapped in the wind. There were a lot of dark clouds.

The door opened behind him. George looked around. He said, "Oh, hello, Jelly."

"Hello, String," Jenny said.

She sat down beside him.

"Something's wrong with Anna," she said. "Anna's in the bedroom with the door shut."

"I know."

"Mama won't let me go in the bedroom. And my jump rope's in there."

"My paper and pencil are in there too."

"And I know a new jump rope rhyme," Jenny said. "It goes like this":

> Jelly Bean, Jelly Bean,
> Ready or not,
> Tell us how many
> Friends you've got.

"Then you count until you miss. One . . . two . . . three—like that. But I can't count my friends because I don't have my jump rope."

"You have a lot of friends."

"I still want to count them." Jenny sighed. "Mama says Anna doesn't feel good."

"I don't feel good either," George admitted.

"I never feel good when something's

wrong with a Bean. Are you still working on your poem?"

"Yes."

"Just make up an awful poem. Get it over with."

"That's what I'm trying to do."

"Want me to do a poem for you? Then we can go downstairs and make dough people. Mama has some scraps. How about this?"

> George wants to go home
> But he don't have a pome.

George shook his head. "You go on," he said. "I'll be down as soon as I can."

"Well, hurry," Jenny said. "It's no fun making dough people by myself."

Jenny went downstairs.

George sat alone for a moment.

Suddenly a raindrop fell beside George. It

left a wet spot as big as a nickel. Another drop fell.

George took a deep breath. His eyes shone.

He bent over his paper. He licked the point of his pencil. He began to write.

Then he jumped up.

George was grinning. He opened the door and started downstairs.

"I did it! I did it!" he cried. "Everybody, I did it!"

Beans at the Table

George burst into the kitchen.

"I did it! I did it!"

Mrs. Bean said, "Don't shout, George."

"Mama! I have to shout! I did my roof poem!"

Mrs. Bean put one finger to her lips.

"Please be quiet, George. Jenny and I think we know what is wrong with Anna."

"But, Mama, don't you want to hear my poem? You gave me the idea for it."

He turned to Jenny.

"Jelly, you want to hear it, don't you?"

Jenny said, "Yes, but not right this minute."

"Well, I'm saying it anyway. I can't stop myself. Here goes:"

When the rain does begin,
George Bean goes in.

He grinned.

"Do you like it? I do. It doesn't have the word *roof* in it, but it is a roof poem."

When the rain does begin,
George Bean goes in.

"Every time I hear it, I like it better."

When the rain does begin—

George stopped. He looked from Jenny to his mother. Neither of them looked happy about his poem.

"Didn't you like it, Jenny?"

"Yes, I liked it."

"Mama?"

"It is a very nice poem, George, but I don't want you to say it to Anna."

"Anna has to hear it, Mama. Anna's the one who started the roof poems. It would make her feel better."

Jenny said, "George, we think Anna's poem is not going in the book."

George said, "What?" His paper dropped to the floor.

Mrs. Bean said, "That's right. We think Anna's poem is not going to be in the book."

George said, "But her poem was better than anybody's."

"We didn't see the others," said Mrs. Bean.

"I know it was better," George said.

"I know it was too," said Jenny. "I just loved it. I wish they had let me pick the poems."

"I do too," said Mrs. Bean.

"How could they not pick Anna's poem?" George asked. "Anna's poem was beautiful."

"I don't know," said Mrs. Bean.

Mrs. Bean dried her eyes on her apron. Then she said, "Well, I better start supper. Your father will be home soon."

"Does Papa know?"

"No, George. I'll tell him later." She looked at them. "Now, children," she said, "when Anna comes out of the bedroom, I don't want to hear one word about poems. I mean it."

"I don't even like poems anymore," Jenny said.

"I don't either," said George.

"Shh! She's coming," Mrs. Bean warned. "Here. Start making dough people. And, remember, not one word about roof poems."

George and Jenny took the dough. They

sat down at the table. They began to roll the dough into balls.

Anna came and stood in the doorway to the kitchen. Her eyes were red and puffy.

"Hi, Anna," Jenny said.

Anna said, "Hi."

"Do you want to make dough people?"

Anna shook her head.

"But we want you to, don't we, George? You make the best dough people of anybody."

George nodded. "I made a dough snake." He held up his strip of dough. He wiggled it to make Anna laugh.

Jenny said, "Please, Anna. It's no fun without you."

"Oh, all right," said Anna. She sat down at the table. She took a piece of dough.

Jenny said, "We can have a play, Anna. Our dough people can be the actors. George's snake can be the announcer."

George put a strip of dough around his snake's neck.

"Look," he said. "My snake has on a necktie. He is ready to announce."

Jenny and Mrs. Bean smiled at the snake in a necktie. Anna smiled too.

But those were not the smiles George wanted. They were not Bean smiles.

He made his snake bow. He made his snake say, "Ladies and gentlemen!"

Beans Together

"Beans! Yoo-hoo! Where are you?"

It was Mr. Bean. He was home from the store.

"We're in the kitchen, Sam. Supper is almost ready."

Mr. Bean stopped in the doorway. He breathed deeply. "Ah, chicken pie," he said. "And I have brought the dessert—fruit."

He brought out four bananas. "They are only a little too ripe," he said.

"Thank your father," Mrs. Bean said.

"Thank you, Papa," they said together.

"You are most welcome."

As Mr. Bean passed the table, he stepped

on a piece of paper. It was the paper with George's poem on it.

He said, "Oh-ho! What is this?"

George said quickly, "Nothing, Papa."

George reached for the piece of paper, but Mr. Bean was too fast.

"Why, George," said Mr. Bean, "it is your roof poem. You have done it at last."

"Not now, Sam," said Mrs. Bean.

"Why not? George is as proud of his poem as we are of ours. Let me read it."

"Later, Sam," said Mrs. Bean.

"I'm sorry, love. I cannot wait."

Mr. Bean cleared his throat and read:

When the rain does begin,
George Bean goes in.

Mr. Bean smiled. "I hope so, George. I hope we all know to come in out of the rain. Now we all have poems."

Mr. Bean sat down at the table. He reached for his napkin. Then he looked up. His smile faded.

"Why, Anna, what is wrong?"

Anna was crying.

She shook her head. "N-nothing," she said.

"It is not nothing. My children do not cry for nothing. Anna, what has happened?"

"Later, Sam," said Mrs. Bean.

"Not later! Now! My beautiful daughter is crying, and I want to know why."

"Well," said Anna, "you will all have to know sometime."

She wiped her eyes. She looked down at the table.

"My poem is not going to be in the book. It was not picked."

Mr. Bean jumped up so fast, he tipped over his chair.

"Anna Bean!" he said.

"I'm s-sorry, Papa."

"Anna Bean, you have nothing to be sorry for! You are the first person in the Bean family to write a poem. That is the most wonderful thing that has ever happened in the history of the Beans."

Mr. Bean put his hand over his heart.

"Children, my father could not read. He could not even write his name. And here, forty years later, is a Bean who can write a poem, a poem as beautiful as a song. That makes me very, very proud."

"But it's not going to be in the book," Anna said.

"Not in this book maybe," said Mr. Bean. "I don't care about this book."

"You don't?"

"No, for if you keep on writing poems, Anna, one day you will be in a book. That's the book I care about."

"Oh, Papa."

Anna ran around the table. She threw her arms around her father's neck.

"I never want to be in a book," Jenny said.

"So what do you want to be?" Mr. Bean said. He was still hugging Anna, but he smiled at Jenny.

"I want to be on the stage."

"And you, George?"

"Well, I don't want to be in a book either. Maybe I'll . . ." George stopped to think. "Maybe I'll build bridges."

"George, I didn't know you were going to build bridges," Jenny said.

"Well, I didn't know you were going on the stage."

"Ah, three famous children," Mr. Bean said. "A poet, an actress, a bridge builder."

He reached out and gathered them into his arms. "What more could any man ask for?"

He breathed deeply.

"Ah, only one thing. Your mother's chicken pie for supper. Get in your seats, Beans," he said.

Jenny, George, and Anna ran to their seats. Mrs. Bean set the chicken pie on the table. Mr. Bean tucked his napkin under his chin.

"Yes," he said, looking around the table, "I am a very happy Bean."

George looked around the table too. Everyone was smiling. And these were Bean smiles!

"We are the luckiest Beans in the world," he said.

And not one single Bean disagreed.

BETSY BYARS'S sharp perceptions and skill at penetrating the inner life of children have made her one of America's most popular and honored writers for young people. Her *Summer of the Swans* was awarded the Newbery Medal, and *The Night Swimmers* won the American Book Award for juvenile fiction in 1980. She is the author of the highly acclaimed Blossom Family Quartet.

Ms. Byars is a licensed pilot and lives in Clemson, South Carolina.

MELODYE ROSALES, illustrator of *Beans on the Roof,* is a graphic designer and artist living in Chicago, Illinois. This is her first book for Delacorte Press.